This book ~~belongs to:~~ *is shared with*

_____

_____

_____

the sunburnt polarbear

to all who call Earth home

© July 2020 Conscious Stories LLC
Book 15

Illustrations by Liesl Bell

Published by
Conscious Stories
350 E. Royal Lane
Suite #150
Irving, TX 75039

www.consciousstories.com

First Edition

ISBN 978-1-943750-35-1

Library of Congress
Control Number:
2020912907

The last 20 minutes of every day are precious.

Dear parents, teachers, and readers,

Like all *Conscious Stories*, this book begins with a simple mindfulness practice to help you connect more deeply with your children in the last 20 minutes of each day.

● When you set your intention to create a calm and connected storytime, then that's what you will get! To help, start your storytime with the **Snuggle Breathing Meditation™**. Read each line aloud and take slow, deep breaths together. This can be very relaxing and help everyone settle.

● At the end of the story, you will find important educational extras. Climate change is a big subject, and to make it accessible to young minds, there is a special page outlining: **What are climate change and global warming?** This speaks about the problem, but we want to be part of the solution! So there are practical action steps that kids can take at home: **Top Tips to Help Polar Bears Thrive**. Also found in the back of the book is a sample **Letter to Politicians** that you can copy and mail to make sure your voice is heard.

● We are the generation that needs to address this global problem. Our kids have the creativity and empathy to make the changes needed. Let's set them up to succeed!

Enjoy Snuggling into Togetherness

An easy breathing meditation

Snuggle Breathing

Our story begins with us breathing together.
Say each line aloud and then
take a slow, deep breath in and out.

Breathing in, I breathe for me.

Breathing in, I breathe for you.

Breathing in, I breathe for us.

Breathing in, I breath for all that surrounds us.

Polar bear moms are
Chitchatting together.
They're awfully worried
About the warm weather.

3

As this heat keeps climbing,

We're getting too hot

To wear all this fur

Or to wander a lot.

We need short summer haircuts,
And wide frilly hats,
Cool sodas to drink,
And sun tanning mats.

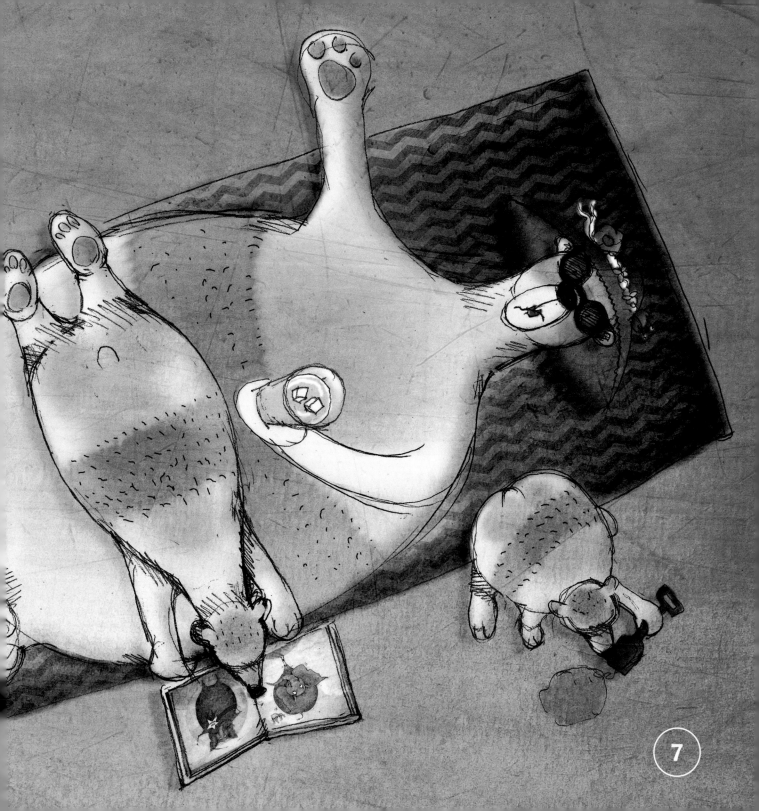

We need factor 100
Sunblock for our tans
And extra-fast spinning
Air cooling fans.

No dinosaurs melt
From the ice when it shrinks.
It's muddy and yucky
And boggy and stinks.

Our white color scheme
Used to be very slick,
But now it stands out
And we look like we're sick.

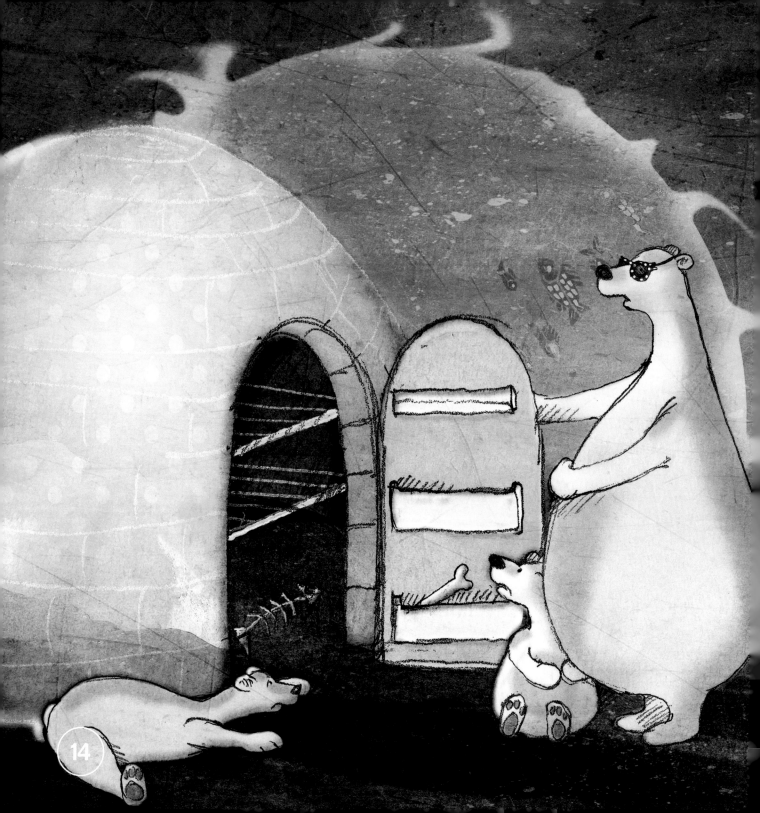

Our favorite foods
Were fresh fish and fat seals.
They left with the ice
Leaving only canned meals.

Perhaps we should wander
down into town
Looking for garbage
To eat or to scrounge.

The North Pole's too hot
For polar bear fun
We're roasting and toasting
Under the sun.

18

Please put in a word
With your own politicians
To make some new laws
And reduce bad emissions.

21

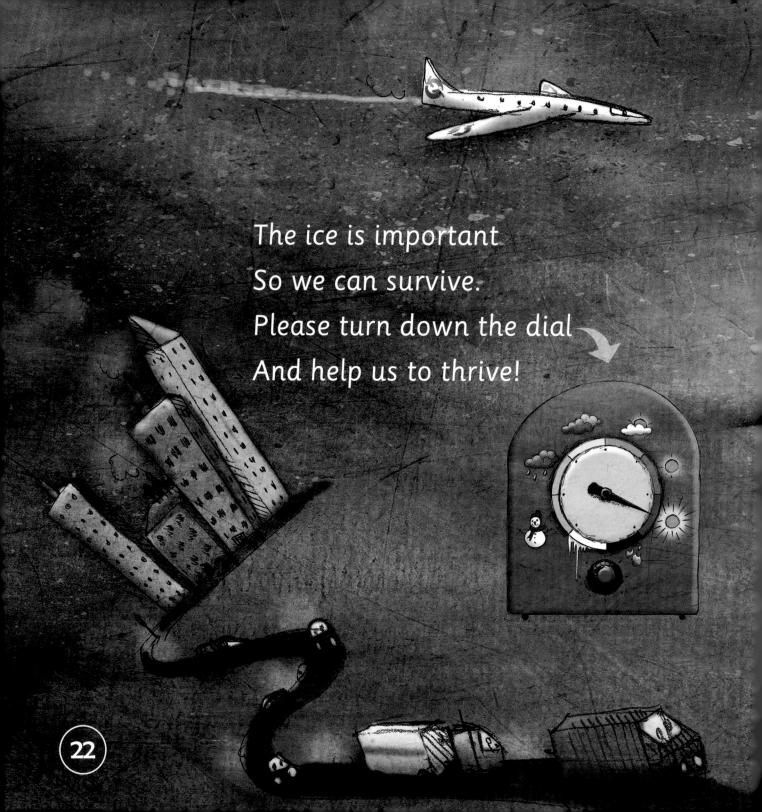

The ice is important
So we can survive.
Please turn down the dial
And help us to thrive!

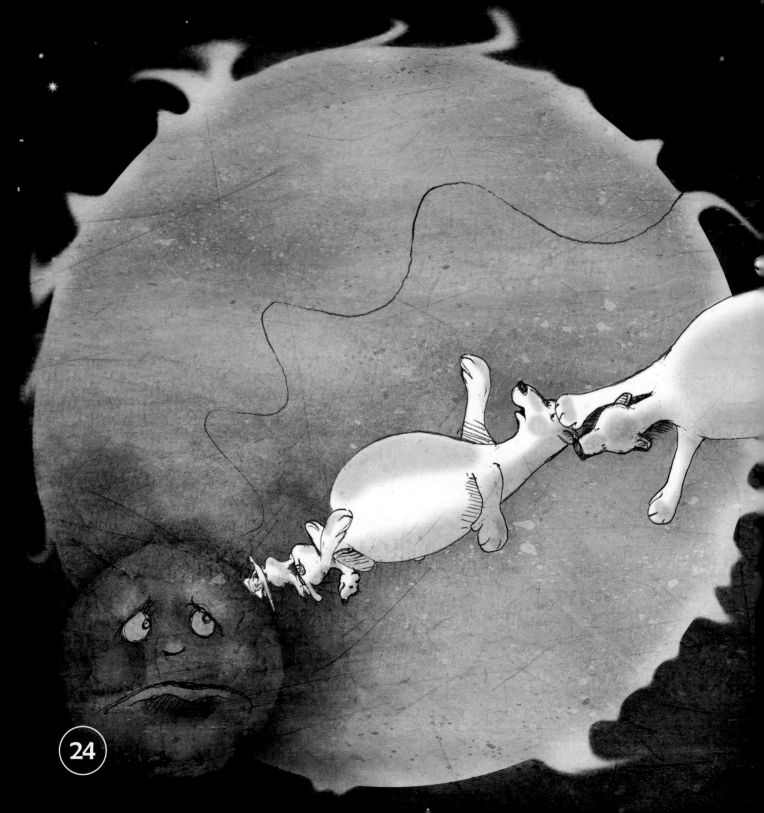

Climate Change is no joke.
The ice caps won't last
Environmental protection
Is needed and fast!

Our homes are shrinking as the icecaps melt. We need your help

- Mama Polar Bear

Climate Change can feel big and scary. Here is a simple explanation of what is going wrong. On the next page you will see how you can help.

Keep breathing.
We can fix this.

Here's the problem

Climate Change and Global Warming

2

Earth's temperature has been perfectly balanced, keeping all living things happy and alive. But, now the temperature is rising, making the Earth feel sick (like when you have a fever).

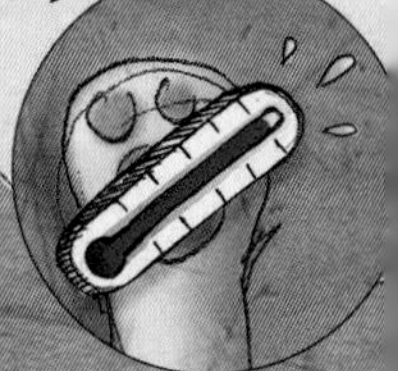

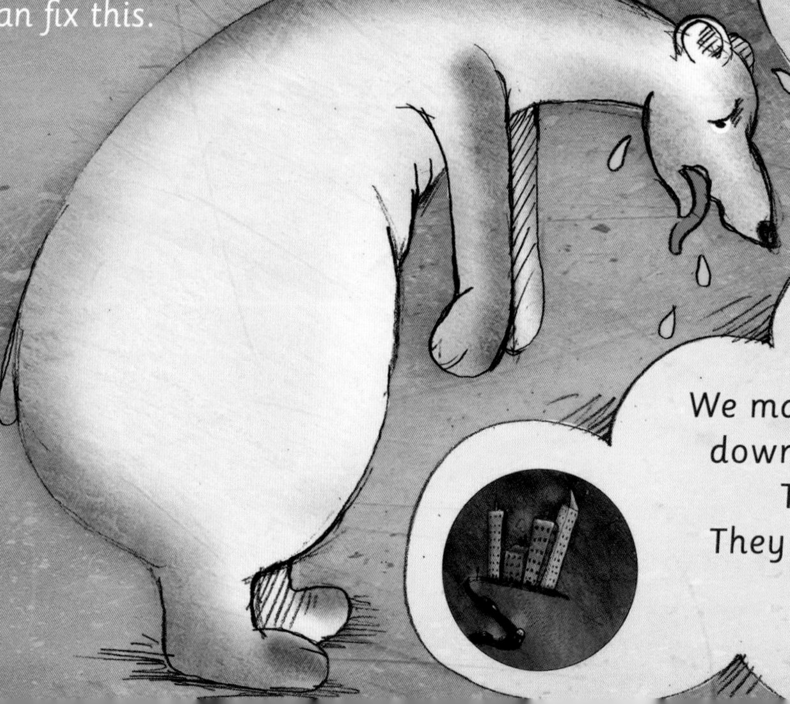

7

We make it worse when we cut down forests to build farms. Trees are like lungs. They help the earth breathe.

3 Warmer temperatures may seem nice, but result in melting ice-caps, rising sea levels, and more extreme weather.

4 Many animals cannot thrive when the temperature changes. Polar bear fur isn't designed for hot, sunny days!

Earth is the home to all living things both big and small - animals (like polar bears), trees, plants, and humans. **1**

START HERE

5 The heat is caused when human pollution creates a thick blanket of dirty air around the earth. This traps too much heat from the sun.

6 A lot of pollution comes from cars, factories and harmful farming practices. It also comes from plastic packaging or littering in your neighborhood.

> **Plastic bottles are not cool. They litter our homes and take hundreds of years to degrade.**
>
> **- Mama Polar Bear**

Here are 6 top-tips to help reduce global warming. When you practice them at home or school you will be helping the polar bears thrive.

Start Today.

Top Tips to Help Polar Bears Thrive

Use less in your house. When you turn off unused lights, water and electronics you save energy and money and help keep the earth cooler.

1

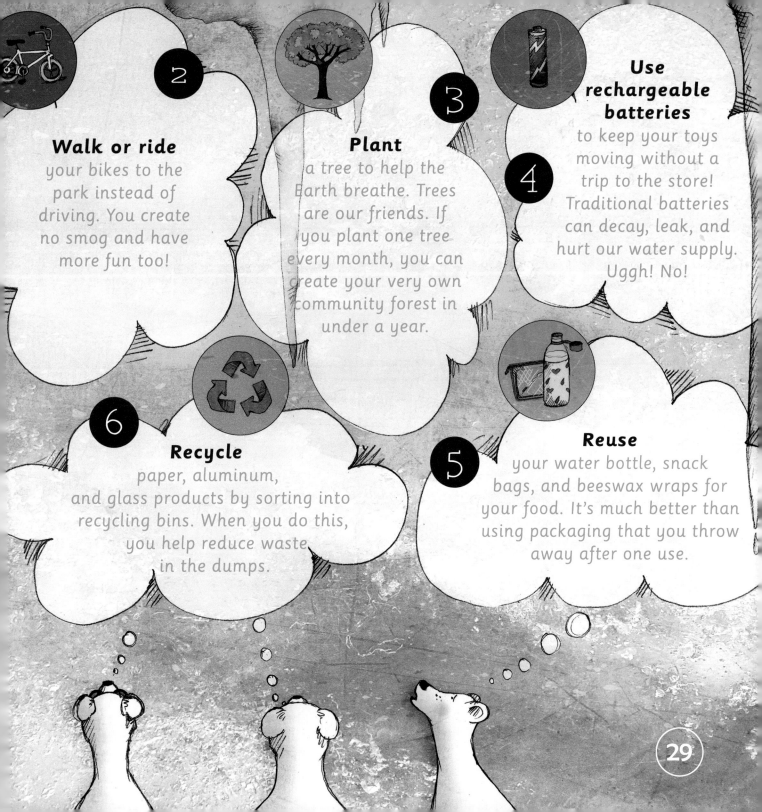

Walk or ride
your bikes to the park instead of driving. You create no smog and have more fun too!

2

Plant
a tree to help the Earth breathe. Trees are our friends. If you plant one tree every month, you can create your very own community forest in under a year.

3

Use rechargeable batteries
to keep your toys moving without a trip to the store! Traditional batteries can decay, leak, and hurt our water supply. Uggh! No!

4

Reuse
your water bottle, snack bags, and beeswax wraps for your food. It's much better than using packaging that you throw away after one use.

5

Recycle
paper, aluminum, and glass products by sorting into recycling bins. When you do this, you help reduce waste in the dumps.

6

the growing collection

The Conscious Bedtime Story Club

snuggling into togetherness

the laughing witch

how diablo became Spirit
Anna Breytenbach & Andrew Newman

the tree of goodness
Andrew Newman

Rolling Thunder finds his herd
Andrew Newman

the elephant who tried to tiptoe

the boy who searched for silence

the dad who didn't know
Andrew Newman

we are circle people
Andrew Newman

the hug who got stuck

the sunburnt polar bear

the fish who searched for water
Andrew Newman

the bee who could not choose her flower
Andrew Newman

a little light

the girl with waterfall eyes
Andrew Newman

the forgetful elephant
Andrew Newman

the prayer who searched for God
Andrew Newman

Discover all available titles at www.consciousstories.com

Conscious Bedtime Stories

A collection of stories with wise and lovable characters who teach spiritual values to your children

Helping you connect more deeply in the last 20 minutes of the day

Stories with purpose

Lovable characters who overcome life's challenges to find peace, love and connection.

Reflective activity pages

Cherish open sharing time with your children at the end of each day.

Simple mindfulness practices

Enjoy easy breathing practices that soften the atmosphere and create deep connection when reading together.

Supportive parenting community

Join a community of conscious parents who seek connection with their children.

Free downloadable coloring pages
Visit www.consciousstories.com

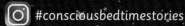 #consciousbedtimestories   @Conscious Bedtime Story Club

Andrew Newman - author

Andrew Newman is the award-winning author and founder of www.ConsciousStories.com, a growing series of bedtime stories purpose-built to support parent-child connection in the last 20 minutes of the day. His professional background includes deep training in therapeutic healing work and mindfulness. He brings a calm yet playful energy to speaking events and workshops, inviting and encouraging the creativity of his audiences, children K-5, parents, and teachers alike.

Andrew has been an opening speaker for Deepak Chopra, a TEDx presenter in Findhorn, Scotland and author-in-residence at the Bixby School in Boulder, Colorado. He is a graduate of The Barbara Brennan School of Healing, a Non-Dual Kabbalistic healer and has been actively involved in men's work through the Mankind Project since 2006. He counsels parents, helping them to return to their center, so they can be more deeply present with their kids.

TED^x   **"Why the last 20 minutes of the day matter"**

Liesl Bell — illustrator

Born and raised in South Africa, Liesl moved to New York where she started her illustration career by creating corporate illustrations for IBM and Xerox's human resources intranet sites. Since then, she has had a line of hand-crafted greeting cards and illustrated numerous educational and private children's books, one of which awarded "This Book Rocks Award" for illustration. Her motto is: Create it with a smile and a wink. She now illustrates full-time in Jeffreys Bay, South Africa where she lives with her young son and two dogs.

www.zigglebell.com

Dear _____

My name is _____. I am _____ years old.
I live in _____.

Climate change is a big problem. Our earth is dying because of global warming.
Extreme weather is causing dangerous storms, droughts, and fires. If we don't
make a change then many people will lose their homes and get sick.

Action is urgently needed.

I am asking you to take responsibility to help.

Please change the laws to:
1. Make climate action a priority across all parts of government.
2. Lower bad emissions by ending support for fossil fuels.
3. Encourage use of clean and renewable energy.

We are doing our part to help in our family, school and neighbourhood.
We are counting on you to start this now!

_____
(Name)

Star Counter

Every time you breathe together and
read aloud, you make a star shine in the
night sky.

Color in a star to count how many
times you have read this book.